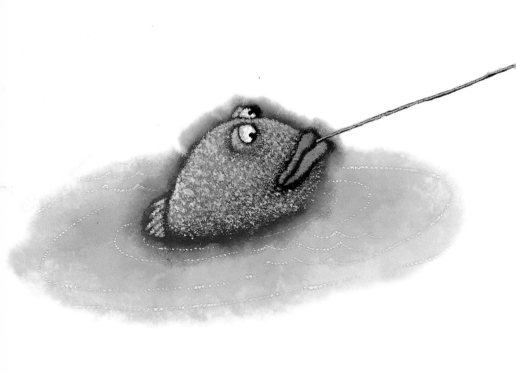

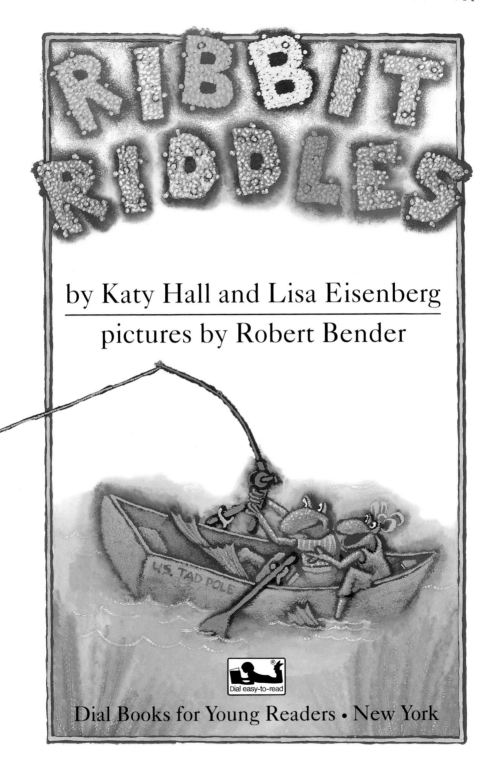

RIBBIT RIDDLES

by Katy Hall and Lisa Eisenberg

pictures by Robert Bender

U.S. TAD POLE

Dial easy-to-read

Dial Books for Young Readers • New York

Published by Dial Books for Young Readers
A division of Penguin Putnam Inc.
345 Hudson Street
New York, New York 10014

Text copyright © 2001 by Kate McMullan and Lisa Eisenberg
Pictures copyright © 2001 by Robert Bender
All rights reserved
Printed in the U.S.A.

The Dial Easy-to-Read logo is a registered trademark of
Dial Books for Young Readers,
a division of Penguin Putnam Inc.
® TM 1,162,718.
1 3 5 7 9 10 8 6 4 2

Library of Congress Cataloging-in-Publication Data
Hall, Katy.
Ribbit riddles/by Katy Hall and Lisa Eisenberg;
pictures by Robert Bender.
p.   cm.
Summary: A collection of riddles and jokes about frogs.
Example: What do little frogs like to eat on a hot summer day?
Hopsicles!
ISBN 0-8037-2525-6
1. Riddles, Juvenile. 2. Frogs—Juvenile humor.
[1. Riddles. 2. Jokes. 3. Frogs—Wit and humor.]
I. Eisenberg, Lisa. II. Bender, Robert, ill. III. Title.
PN6371.5.H3482   2001
818'.5402—dc21   99-089174

Reading Level 2.5

The art for this book was created using
cell-vinyl paint on layers of acetate.

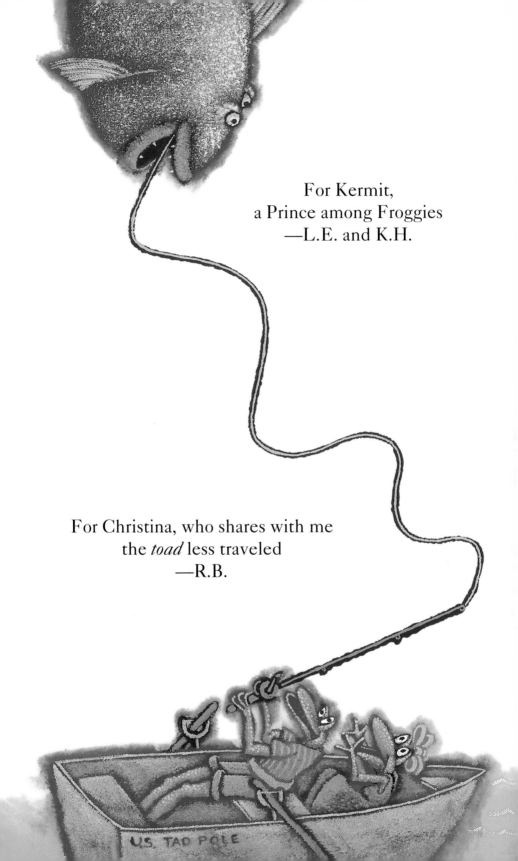

For Kermit,
a Prince among Froggies
—L.E. and K.H.

For Christina, who shares with me
the *toad* less traveled
—R.B.

U.S. TAD POLE

What do little frogs like to eat
on a hot summer day?

Hopsicles!

What happened when the
frog left his car in the
No Parking zone?

His car was toad!

Which froggy was king of
rock 'n' roll?

Elvis Presleap!

What's mean and green and
picks on little tadpoles?

A bully-frog!

What happened when the
Frog Prince married the Frog
Princess?

They lived hoppily ever after!

Who brings baskets of eggs to little frogs in the spring?

The Easter Ribbit!

What did one tadpole say to
the other?

"Water you doing?"

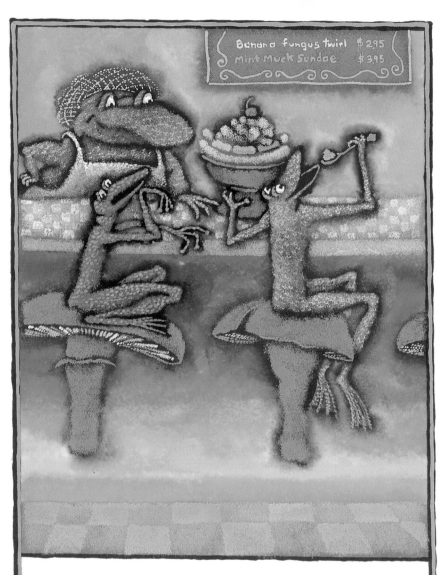

Where do frogs like to sit
at the ice cream parlor?

On toadstools!

Why do frogs make such great
baseball players?

They are good at catching flies!

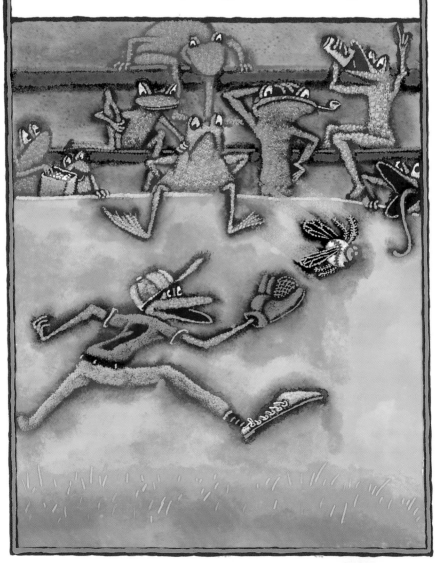

What do frogs like to eat for breakfast?

Hop-Tarts!

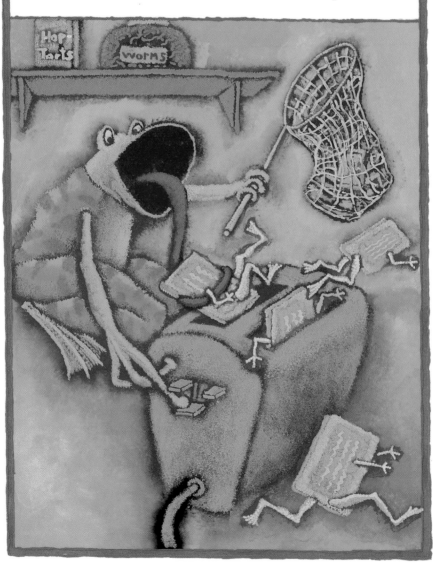

Which ballet is the froggy favorite?

Swamp Lake!

What did the frog ask for
at the fast-food restaurant?

A quarter-ponder and an order of flies!

What do little froggies play
house with?

Dollywogs!

19

How did the frog look in his
new outfit?

Toadally cool!

What do you call a bunch of froggy footprints?

A website!

Why did the frog say "Tweet"?

She was speaking a foreign tongue!

What did the foot doctor tell
the frog?

"You need a hop-eration!"

Why should you never take a
check from a frog?

It might bounce!

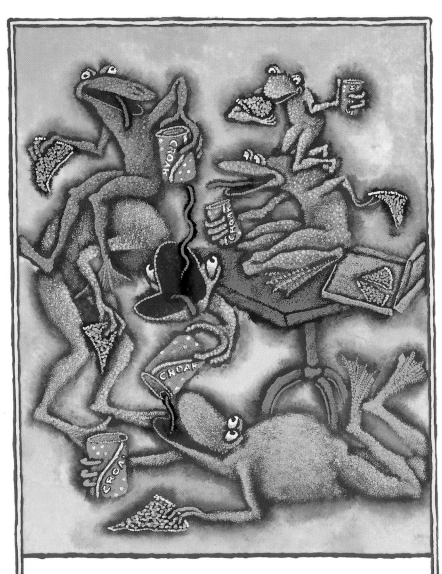

What do froggies drink with
their pizza?

Croak!

What do you call a tadpole's
hairpiece?

A pollywig!

What do you call froggy sandals?

Open-toad shoes!

How does a froggy steer a canoe?

With a lily pad-dle!

Why didn't the frog like the trout?

There was something fishy about him!

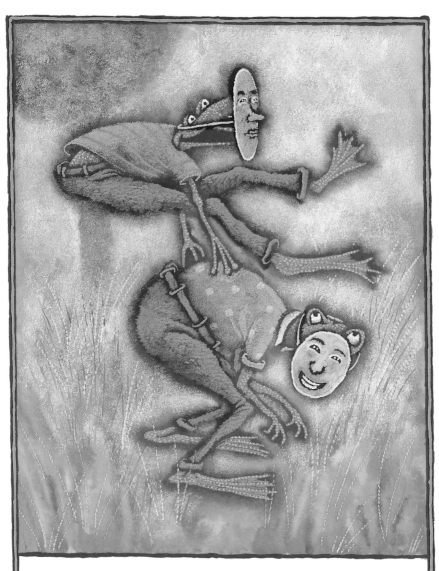

What game do little frogs play
at recess?

Leap people!

What did one toad say to the
other toad?

"Wart's up?"

What did the cowboy frogs eat
at the big barbecue?

Spare ribbits!

What goes dot-dot-dot-croak?

Morse toad!

What do you get if you cross a pig with a frog?

A ham-phibian!

Which froggy won the Olympic
gold medal?

The tadpole-vaulter!

What's green and tough and
guards the house?

A watch-frog!

Why did the frog go to jail?

For robbing the riverbank!

What do you get if you cross a tadpole and a parrot?

An animal that says "Pollywog a cracker!"

Which froggy was a Viking?

Leap Eriksson!

What country do frogs come from?

Greenland!

$13.99

DATE			